Nine Lives

BEN M. BAGLIO

Nine Lives
Emerald, Amber, and Jet

Illustrated by Bill Geldart

AN
APPLE
PAPERBACK

SCHOLASTIC INC.

New York   Toronto   London   Auckland   Sydney
Mexico City   New Delhi   Hong Kong   Buenos Aires

ISBN 0-439-32257-X

12 11 10 9 8 7 6 5 4 3 2 1   1 2 3 4 5 6/0

Printed in the U.S.A.   40
First Scholastic printing, November 2001

To Hercules, a big cuddly cat who was
loved right to the white tip of his tail

Nine Lives

Bracken is a large tortoiseshell cat who lives with the Bradman family on Liberty Street. Bracken lives a comfortable life and spends much of her time snoozing away in her basket in the Bradmans' house.

Mr. Bradman — Dad — used to be a lawyer, but he gave up this career for his real passion — gardening. He found Bracken abandoned in an alley two years ago when she was just a tiny kitten.

Mrs. Bradman — Mom — is a bank manager. Unlike Mr. Bradman, she loves her indoor office job.

Elsie Jennings — Grandma — is Mrs. Bradman's mom. She lives a few doors away on Liberty Street. She may be older than 65, but Elsie has lots of get-up-and-go and enjoys being with children. That's why she loves her job as the local school crossing guard.

Tom Bradman is thirteen years old and has an early morning job as a paperboy. He and his younger sister, Ellie, love animals. They always make a big fuss over Bracken and their six-year-old golden retriever, Lottie.

Ellie Bradman is ten years old. She's always coming up with great plans and ideas — which is good . . . because earlier this year Bracken had her first litter. She became the proud mom of nine assorted bundles of fur.

Nine kittens, nine very different lives. The Bradmans know they can't keep the kittens, but they're determined that all nine go to the very best homes — homes to suit each very special personality.

Emerald

1

Emerald woke with a start. *What was that?* The mailbox had rattled and something had thudded onto the doormat. *It must be Tom delivering the paper.*

She stood up and stretched, arching her back and spreading her claws.

Then she jumped down from the kitchen chair and scampered along the hallway to the front door. She was right — there was a news-paper lying on the mat.

Emerald pushed the cat flap half-open with her nose. She blinked her bright green eyes in the early morning sunlight. "Hello, Tom," she meowed.

Thirteen-year-old Tom Bradman bent down and peered at the little dark gray face that appeared through the cat flap. "Hello, Emerald." Tom smiled as the rest of Emerald's small furry body followed. He knelt down and stroked her silky fur.

Emerald rubbed her head against Tom's legs. She liked Tom. She had been born in his family's house, just a few doors down from George's apartment on Liberty Street. Her mom, Bracken, was the Bradmans' family cat.

Now Emerald lived with George. She had grown very fond of him, but she was glad to see Tom every day.

Tom tickled Emerald under her chin. She purred loudly to let him know she liked it.

"Well," said Tom, "I'd better continue my paper route." He picked up newspapers each day from Angie and Steve. They owned the corner grocery store next door to George's apartment.

Emerald liked Angie and Steve. They were friendly and they laughed and joked a lot. They always made a fuss over Emerald whenever she visited their store to see her brother Jet, who lived there with them.

Tom stood up and heaved his heavy newspaper bag onto his shoulder. "See you tomorrow," he said, and he began to go down the stairs to the street.

But Emerald wasn't ready to say good-bye to Tom just yet. "I'm coming with you," she meowed, winding herself in and out of his legs.

"Hey!" he cried, clutching the railing just in time before Emerald tripped him. "I don't want to end up in a heap at the bottom of the stairs. Go back home, Emerald."

"But I'm enjoying myself," Emerald meowed. Now that she was six months old, she was allowed outside the apartment. She'd had to stay indoors when she was younger. It was much more fun being free to explore. There were so many places to hide — and things to chase and pounce on.

Emerald would go home later. She walked along the street beside Tom, wanting to play. She walked in front of him, then behind him — then in front of him again.

"Stop it, Emerald!" Tom said with a laugh. "Let me finish my route or I'll be late for school." He took another newspaper out of his bag, folded it, and pushed it into a mailbox.

Just then, Emerald heard her name being called.

"Emerald! Emerald! Where are you?"

It was George's voice. Emerald thought about ignoring it. She didn't really want to leave Tom yet — she was having fun. But she did feel hungry.

Tom had heard George calling Emerald, too. He bent down and gave her one last stroke. "Off you go, Emerald," he said, smiling. "George is looking for you." Then he turned around and continued walking.

Emerald meowed a good-bye and then she was off, running back along the street and up the steep steps to George's apartment. She looked up at George, who was waiting in the doorway for her.

"Here I am," she meowed, rubbing her head against his baggy pants.

George's gray hair hung down over his forehead as he bent forward. "I wondered where you went," he said as his fingers scratched the top of Emerald's head.

Emerald followed George along the hall and into the cozy yellow kitchen, where a dishful of food was waiting for her. It smelled delicious!

"I'm going to have to keep you in if you're going to wander too far," said George, watching Emerald as she wolfed down her breakfast. "Have you been following Tom again?"

Emerald continued eating, but she had heard his warning. She looked at him out of the corner of her eye. *Does he mean it? Would he really keep me indoors and not let me out to explore?* she wondered.

George shook his head worriedly. "I guessed you would grow into a lively cat, but I didn't realize you would be so adventurous," he said.

Emerald stopped eating and looked up at George's kind, wrinkled face. "I can't help wanting to explore," she meowed. She certainly didn't want to be kept inside the apartment forever. That would be terrible!

After she'd finished eating, Emerald took a short nap, then went to find George. She found him busy shaving in the bathroom. Now that she'd had a nap, Emerald felt like playing again. She leaped up onto the sink and sat in front of the big mirror. A tube of tooth-

paste lay nearby. Emerald decided to pounce
on it. A long squiggle of white paste oozed
out.

"Stop it, Emerald!" George said. He dried
his face and went to his bedroom to put on his
socks and shoes.

"But I want to play," Emerald meowed, following him. She decided to bite George's
socks as he put them on.

"Stop it, Emerald!" he said again.

But when George tied his shoelaces, she couldn't resist pouncing on them.

"Emerald!" George said sternly.

Emerald paused and looked up at George. He sounded annoyed. But she saw he was smiling, so she pounced on the laces again.

"Here, play with this," George said, laughing. He threw Emerald's favorite orange plastic ball across the room.

Emerald chased the ball all around the apartment, pouncing on it — then hitting it to make it roll again. But she didn't like playing by herself. "Will you play with me?" she meowed.

But George was busy reading the newspaper in the living room now and didn't answer her.

Emerald decided to climb the living room curtains. She leaped at them, her claws digging deep into the flowery material. Then slowly she climbed toward the ceiling. She loved doing this!

"Hey! Emerald!" said George, hurriedly putting down his paper. "Stop it!"

This time he wasn't smiling — he was frowning. He came over and lifted Emerald off of the curtain and put her firmly on the floor.

Emerald crept under the table. She hated it when George was annoyed. She decided to go and explore outside again.

Pushing her way out through the cat flap, Emerald trotted back down the steps onto the sidewalk. Just then, she heard a scuffling sound behind one of the big garbage cans. She went to investigate.

Suddenly, a mouse shot out from behind the cans. Seeing Emerald, it froze in surprise. Emerald's eyes widened. *Oh, what fun!* she thought. Whiskers twitching, she prepared to pounce. But she wasn't quick enough. The mouse darted away. Emerald hadn't had much practice at catching mice yet. "I'll catch you next time," she meowed.

After playing all morning, Emerald went back home to take a nap. George had settled down on the sofa to watch the afternoon movie on TV. Emerald snoozed on his lap.

When the movie was over, George gently lifted her off his knee and stood up. "It's time I went to work," he said.

Emerald opened a lazy eye. She didn't know what "work" was, but she knew that George left her alone for a long time while he went out. She often wondered where he went.

She followed him into the hallway where he put on his coat.

"Be good," he said as he closed the front door behind him.

Emerald looked at the closed door and then around the empty apartment. She didn't feel like being inside on her own again. Suddenly, she had a bright idea. *I know!* she thought. *I'll follow George and find out where he goes every day!*

She pushed her way through the cat flap, silently walked down the stairs, then looked down the street to see which way George had gone. She spotted him as he disappeared around the corner onto the next street.

Emerald ran after him. As she passed the corner grocery store, she saw that the door was open, so she peered inside. Steve was busy serving a customer and there was no sign of Jet. Emerald turned and ran.

By now, George was a long way ahead. He was walking very fast. The street he had turned onto was much busier and noisier than Liberty Street. Emerald dodged in and out of the legs of people rushing along.

Bang! Emerald jumped as a car door slammed nearby.

Vroom! She darted into a store doorway as a car sped past. She could feel her heart beating very fast inside her chest.

A little girl stopped to stroke her. "What a pretty little cat," said the girl.

Emerald usually loved attention, but she had to keep up with George. "Can't stop!" she meowed as she darted between the girl's legs and escaped. She felt the wind whistling through her whiskers as she ran faster, trying to catch up with George.

As she ran, Emerald spotted an elderly woman dressed in a big, white coat and carrying a large round sign on a long stick. It was Tom's grandmother, Elsie Jennings. Emerald had seen Mrs. Jennings in that coat before. She had sometimes worn it when she'd popped into the Bradmans' house, when Emerald lived there.

Just then, Mrs. Jennings held out her big sign — and the traffic stopped! Amazed, Emerald stopped to watch as she led a crowd of children to the other side of the street.

On her way back, Mrs. Jennings noticed Emerald. "Hello," she said, bending down to stroke the kitten. "It's Emerald, isn't it? I'd recognize those beautiful green eyes anywhere."

Emerald rubbed her face against Mrs. Jennings's hand. "Thank you," she purred. She decided she had time to let Mrs. Jennings stroke her.

"You're a long way from home," said Mrs. Jennings. "You'll get trampled on, or get run over on this busy street. Let me take you home." She tried to pick Emerald up.

Emerald shied away. "I'm not ready to go home yet. I'm following George," she meowed, then turned to continue running. She was just in time to spot George walking into a large building. The enormous glass doors at the entrance were surrounded by bright lights. A long line of people were lining up to go inside.

Why are all those people waiting to go inside? Emerald wondered. *And how come George didn't have to wait?* She was just about to follow George and find out when an enormous truck thundered toward her. Emerald's hair stood on end! She forgot all about following George. All she wanted was to be curled up safely on the sofa in George's apartment.

She dashed out onto the street in a panic, dodging past Mrs. Jennings and the little girl who had stopped to stroke her. She ran around the corner onto Liberty Street, not stopping to see Angie and Steve or Jet. She leaped up the stairs and through the cat flap, then lay panting on the mat inside the door, her heart beating fast.

After a while, Emerald wandered into the kitchen and crunched on a few fish-flavored cat treats in her bowl. That made her feel much better. She decided that, despite her scare, the adventure had been worth it. *I've found out where George goes every day,* she thought. *Next time I'll find out what he does there.*

Emerald made up her mind. She would follow George again tomorrow.

2

The next day, George left the apartment much later — it was almost dark. Emerald had heard George tell a friend on the phone that he was "working the evening shift" today.

Even better, Emerald thought. Nobody would see a dark gray kitten at night!

She followed George as closely as she could, keeping in the shadows at the side of the street.

As George was passing the corner grocery store, he pushed open the door and went in. Emerald slipped into the store behind him.

Jet came to meet her and they greeted each other, touching noses and rubbing faces.

"Quick!" Emerald hissed to her brother. "I don't want George to see me. I'm following him to find out what he does when he goes to work in the evening."

While George was talking and laughing with Angie, Jet led Emerald to a cardboard box at the side of the store. "If you hide behind here, they won't notice you," he meowed.

Emerald and Jet sat watching George.

After a few minutes, he left the store and Emerald slipped out behind him.

"Thanks, Jet!" she meowed, then followed George around the corner and onto the busy street.

But at this time of day, it was much less busy. There weren't so many people around — and there was less traffic to be frightened of. No one stopped to stroke Emerald. And Mrs. Jennings was nowhere to be seen.

The large building surrounded by lights came into view. Now that it was dark outside, the lights looked even brighter and more exciting. Again, George ignored the line of people and walked right in through the big glass doors.

Emerald stared up at the bright lights and the enormous posters on the walls. One showed a huge ship, and another showed the full moon shining down on an old house.

"I can't wait to see this movie," said a man in the line of people, waiting to go in.

"Neither can I," said the woman with him. She shivered. "It's going to be really scary."

Emerald looked up. She'd seen the couple who were talking before. They were friends of George.

"Nothing scares me," said the man, grinning.

"Lots of things scare me!" meowed Emerald. Just then, the glass doors were opened wide and the line began to shuffle slowly into the building. Emerald crept past the line and went inside. There were more bright lights past the glass doors and a woman sitting behind a counter, looking very busy. But there was no sign of George.

"*Oh, no!*" meowed Emerald to herself. "*What should I do now?*" She decided to hide in a corner and see if George would come back. When the couple she had heard talking outside came in, they were still talking about scary movies.

Suddenly, Emerald spotted George coming through some swinging doors. *How strange!* she thought. It looked as though the room he was coming from was very dark!

George saw the couple and grinned. "Hi, you two," he said. "Are you looking forward to being frightened out of your wits?"

"Is this movie as good as they say?" asked the man.

"It's great!" said George. "It's one of my favorites!"

"Most movies are your favorites!" laughed the woman. "That's why you work at the movie theater!"

"True!" laughed George.

"Oh," Emerald meowed quietly. "A movie theater?"

George turned and walked back through the swinging doors into the dark room. Emerald wasted no time. She shot silently from her corner and through the doors just before they shut.

The dark room was huge! And it was warm. Emerald loved feeling warm. She loved all the warm spots at home, like in front of the fire, or snuggled up on George's knee, or in a patch of sunlight on the carpet.

Emerald didn't mind the dark, either. She

could still see everything that was going on. There were rows and rows of seats, all facing the same way, with people sitting in them. George was walking up and down the aisle shining a flashlight in front of him, then shining the flashlight at the seats so the people could see which ones were empty.

Emerald watched George's friends from outside go and sit near the front. Then George went out through the swinging doors again.

Emerald decided to stick around to see what would happen next. She found an empty seat in the back. It was soft and velvety, so she pushed her front paws into it, up and down, over and over again. It felt great! It reminded her of when she used to press her paws into her mom's tummy when she wanted some milk.

Emerald settled down and looked around her. Now she was higher up and found she was facing an enormous screen. It was like the

TV in George's apartment, only much, much bigger.

Suddenly, there was loud music, and pictures started flashing across the screen.

A scary-looking house, like the one on the poster outside, came into view. The moon was shining in a dark sky and gray clouds were moving across it.

Emerald was enjoying herself. It was very warm and cozy here. Slowly, her eyes began to droop. All this excitement had worn her out! She decided to have a quick snooze.

Crash! Emerald woke with a start. At first she wondered where on earth she was. Then she saw the huge screen and remembered. On the screen, a storm was raging. Thunder and lightning were crashing around the spooky house in the movie. A man was creeping around outside the house. Emerald thought he looked a bit frightened!

She yawned and stretched, then decided to

explore a little more. She jumped down from her seat and silently crept along the aisle beside the rows of seats. She looked at the people watching the movie. Lots of them were gripping the sides of their seats or holding onto the person next to them. Some were staring. Some had their mouths wide open. Some were chewing their fingernails. *How strange!* she thought.

Emerald wondered if George's friends were scared, too. She decided to look for them. But where were they? It would be hard to find them in such a big place. Then she remembered that they were somewhere near the front. She would creep toward the screen and try to find them.

Emerald was halfway to the front when something made her look up. She blinked. Then she blinked again. Right in the middle of the screen was an enormous, dark gray cat, just like her!

The cat stalked across the screen. Emerald's

eyes opened wide. It was huge! "I wonder why it's in the movie," she meowed, but nobody heard her.

The music in the background started getting louder and faster. It made Emerald want to dance. So she chased her tail and jumped on pieces of popcorn that people had dropped on the floor. But no one seemed to notice her. What was going on?

Emerald looked up at the cat on the screen. She decided it would be fun to copy it. When the cat on the screen stretched, Emerald stretched. When it crept across the screen, Emerald crept slowly toward it. She crept closer and closer.

Then the dark gray cat on the screen vanished.

"Where did it go?" Emerald meowed. Perhaps if she jumped onto a seat she'd get a better view. But there didn't seem to be any empty ones nearby. So Emerald decided to jump onto the back of an occupied one.

Suddenly, the people in the row behind began to gasp and scream. Emerald crouched low in fright and gripped the seat tightly with her claws.

What had happened?

She ran along the row, behind people's heads, trying to see what had scared everyone. And then she saw that everyone was looking at her!

"It's come to life!" shouted a woman. "The ghost cat in the movie — it's here — in the theater!"

Emerald was pleased with herself. *I must have pretended to be the cat on the screen very well!* she thought. *Perhaps I'll do it some more!* She began to pretend she was the cat on the screen again, copying its movements as she walked along the backs of the seats.

Now everyone was noticing Emerald pretending to be the dark gray screen cat. People screamed and shouted all around her, and the noise began to frighten her. Emerald didn't know what to do.

Then above all the other shouts, Emerald heard a familiar one. "Emerald!"

It was George! Emerald meowed back to him, "Help me, George!" Then she jumped down from the seat back and raced into the shadows toward him.

"The ghost cat's disappeared!" she heard someone say as George scooped her up.

"That was weird!" someone else said.

"And scary!"

Just then the movie finished, and when the lights came on, George slipped outside with Emerald and took her into a small, dark room.

"Emerald, how on earth did you get here?" George said, shaking his head. "I'm going to be in big trouble now — you've scared the audience half to death!"

Suddenly, the door burst open and a red-faced man stormed in. When he saw Emerald, his eyes widened. "Who does that cat belong to?" he boomed.

"Me, Mr. Skinner," said George quietly.

Mr. Skinner went even redder and more angry-looking. "George," he shouted. "I want a word with you in my office. Now!"

3

I don't think I like him, thought Emerald, as George followed Mr. Skinner out of the room.

Emerald crept under a table, feeling very worried for George. It was her fault he was in trouble. *I wish I hadn't been so curious. I wish I'd stayed at home in the apartment,* she thought.

Slowly, the noise of people talking about the ghost cat lessened, as everyone went home. Emerald began to feel drowsy. After a few minutes her eyes closed and she fell fast asleep.

A bright, flashing light woke Emerald up. "Emerald," George was whispering. "Where are you? Come out. It's all right. I'll take you home."

"I'm here," Emerald meowed. But she stayed hidden in her dark corner. She was worried that angry Mr. Skinner might be with him.

George's flashlight beam slowly came nearer. It flashed around Emerald, across her, then it stopped right on her. "So there you are, you little troublemaker!" he said.

Emerald couldn't decide whether he sounded angry or not, but she knew she could trust him. She would be safe with him. He would take her home. "I'm so glad to see you, George," she meowed.

A few minutes later, she was tucked inside his coat, snuggled down under his chin. She purred as George walked briskly along the main road and around the corner onto Liberty Street. Everything was very still and quiet. Emerald guessed it must be the middle of the night. George climbed up the stairs and unlocked the door of his apartment.

"I'm keeping you in for the rest of the night," he said as he put Emerald on the floor. "We don't want any more trouble."

She watched him lock the cat flap. "I don't mind — I've had enough adventures for one day!" she meowed, wrapping herself around George's legs. "I'm sorry if I got you into trouble."

But George didn't stroke her or pick her up. Emerald thought he seemed upset.

Early the next morning, when the newspaper thudded onto the mat, George and Emerald were already awake. They both hurried over to the door and George opened it. Tom was standing outside.

"Hello!" he said to George. "I didn't expect to see you up so early! I was waiting to say good morning to Emerald!"

Emerald purred.

"I couldn't sleep," said George. "So I thought I might as well get up early for a change."

Emerald looked up at George. He certainly did look very tired. And it was all her fault.

When Tom had gone, George went and slumped in an armchair, looking miserable. Emerald jumped up and sat on the arm of the chair beside him. She was glad when George stroked the top of her head and began to talk.

"My manager was so angry," he said sadly. "He told me I can't work at the movie theater anymore. He said I shouldn't have let my cat follow me to work. I told him I didn't know you were there until you suddenly leaped up and terrified everyone."

"I'm sorry!" Emerald meowed. She rubbed her head against his hand. She hoped he could tell she was sorry.

"I loved that job," said George, "because I got to see all the latest movies."

Emerald crouched low and nuzzled against his shoulder. "I hope you'll forgive me," she meowed. "I couldn't bear it if you didn't."

George sat miserably in the apartment all day. Then as it began to grow dark, the phone rang.

George went into the hall and picked up the receiver. "Hello," he said quietly. "Oh . . . yes, sir . . ."

Emerald sat down next to him to listen.

"Oh," said George, looking surprised. "Really?" He began to sound excited. "Thank you, sir."

Who was it on the phone? What was George getting excited about?

"Oh, yes, sir," said George. He beamed down at Emerald. "I'm sure she will. I'll see you as soon as I can. Good-bye."

He put the receiver down and rushed over

and picked Emerald up. "Good job, Emerald!" he said.

Emerald purred. She liked it when she made George happy, but what had she done?

"That was Mr. Skinner, my manager," said George, excitedly. "He said that there is a huge line building up outside the movie theater to see the horror film. All the people that saw you last night have told their friends. They loved you because you made the movie so much more scary. And now everyone wants to see if the ghost cat will show up again!" George chuckled. "They say seeing you was the best part!"

Emerald snuggled against George's shoulder.

"So," George went on, "Mr. Skinner wants me to take you to the theater right now, so you can pretend to be the ghost cat again."

Emerald meowed loudly. She had never thought of herself as a scary cat before, but the more she thought about it, the more she liked the idea!

"I'd love to," she purred. "It'll be fun!"

"But we can't tell anyone," said George. He put Emerald down and put on his coat. "It has to be a secret. And I'll have to hide you in my coat as we go past the line," he said, opening the door. "Come on, Emerald. We have to hurry!"

Emerald scampered behind George as he ran down the steps, along to the corner and past the store where Jet sat in the doorway washing himself. Emerald stopped to talk to her brother.

"Where are you going, looking so pleased with yourself?" meowed Jet.

"I'm going to be the star of the show," meowed Emerald proudly. "Only it's a secret."

"Star of the show? Secret?" meowed Jet. "What are you talking about?"

"I'll tell you about it later," meowed Emerald.

"Come on, Emerald," called George. "We can't keep your audience waiting!"

With her head and tail held high, Emerald caught up with George. Then they hurried off to the theater.

As they got closer, George picked Emerald up and hid her in his coat. They went past the long line of excited people and through the big glass doors.

The manager was just coming out of his office. He caught George by the elbow. "Do you have her?" he hissed.

George opened the top of his coat and Emerald saw Mr. Skinner peering in at her.

The manager grinned. "And do you think she'll do it?"

"Let's hope so," whispered George, kissing Emerald on the top of her head.

"You'll see," Emerald meowed quietly.

Some time later, Emerald crept silently into the dark. All the seats were full and everyone was watching the movie, wondering if they would see the ghost cat, like yesterday's audience. Little did they know that Emerald was about to frighten them out of their wits! And this time, she wouldn't be scared by their screams and shouts. She was going to have the time of her life!

Emerald crept like a shadow toward the front. She lay low, ready to leap out at exactly the right moment.

As the screen cat disappeared, Emerald jumped on top of a seat back and began to make her way along the row. What noise the people made!

As she had done the night before, Emerald jumped into the shadows when she reached the end of the row, then went to hide with George until all the people had left.

Soon afterward, Mr. Skinner burst into George's little room again. But this time he didn't look angry — he looked very happy.

"Fantastic job — er — Emerald!" he said with a beaming smile. "You're a star!"

Then he turned to George. "I'd like you to have your job back, George," he said. "With a pay raise — as long as Emerald comes with you!"

"Of course!" laughed George. "Emerald

loved having everyone watch her. I'm sure she'd like to do it every night!"

Emerald purred and rubbed her face against George in agreement. She liked being the star of the show. But even better — she got to go to work with George!

Amber

1

Amber scampered toward the back door. She had heard Mr. Bradman's voice and that meant Lottie, the Bradman's golden retriever, would be home from her walk. Amber found Lottie and Mr. Bradman in the kitchen.

"I'm glad you're back," Amber purred happily. Lottie ran over to Amber and licked the kitten's nose. "We went on a great walk!" she barked.

Amber looked up at Lottie's friendly face. "I wish I could have gone," she meowed. "Where did you go?"

"Down by the river," Lottie barked.

"I can see that!" Amber meowed, looking at Lottie's big soft-padded paws. "Your paws are all muddy."

Mr. Bradman finished taking off his muddy boots, then grabbed an old towel from under the sink. "Come on, Lottie," he said. "Let's clean you up."

Lottie went over to Mr. Bradman, Amber trotting happily underneath her, running in and out of her legs. Amber knew that Lottie would be careful not to step on her friend.

Tom was sitting at the kitchen table doing his homework. He laughed. "Those two are great together, aren't they?" he said. "And in a funny way they look alike because their coats are such a similar color."

"Yes, and you'd think Amber was a puppy,

not a kitten, the way she behaves!" chuckled Mr. Bradman.

"I wish I were!" meowed Amber.

"Lottie's so good with all the kittens," said Tom. "But Amber's definitely her favorite."

"Of course I am," purred Amber.

"They'll miss each other when we find Amber a new home," said Mr. Bradman.

"But I don't need a new home," meowed Amber. "I'm very happy here, thank you."

Mr. Bradman began to wipe Lottie's paws with the towel. Amber pounced on one corner and tugged at it with her claws.

Bracken was sitting in the cat basket in the corner, washing Amber's sister Clove.

"Don't be a nuisance, dear," she meowed at Amber.

"I'm not," meowed Amber. "Lottie loves having me around. But I wish I were allowed to go for a walk with her."

"Cats don't go for walks," Bracken meowed back.

"Why not?" asked Amber.

But Bracken was too busy cleaning behind Clove's ears to answer.

It wasn't fair! Amber thought. *Why couldn't a kitten go for a walk?* "In that case, I wish I were a dog!" she meowed.

"Don't be silly," meowed Bracken. "Anyway, you're too young to be allowed out."

When Mr. Bradman had finished cleaning Lottie, she went to her water bowl to have a drink. Her long, floppy tongue lapped the water noisily. Amber ran over and put her front paws on the opposite side of the bowl. Copying Lottie, she lapped away with her tiny tongue.

Tom laughed, then got up from the table and reached into the cabinet. "Watch this, Dad," he said, getting some dog treats. "Here, Lottie," he called.

Lottie left her water and ran to Tom, her tail wagging furiously. Amber trotted at her heels.

"Lottie, sit," said Tom. Lottie sat down. Amber sat beside her.

"Good girl, Lottie," said Tom. "And good girl, Amber!"

"Woof!" barked Lottie.

"Woof!" meowed Amber.

"Shake paws," said Tom. Lottie lifted a front paw and shook Tom's hand. Amber did the same.

"Good girl, Lottie," said Tom, giving her a dog biscuit. "Good girl, Amber," he said, giving her one, too.

Amber loved them. They were much more tasty than cat treats — and much bigger!

The next morning, when Tom came home from his paper route, he found Lottie gnawing at a large bone with the tiny golden kitten beside her, as usual. Amber's teeth weren't fully grown yet, but she was copying everything that Lottie did.

Lottie stopped chewing when she saw Tom, so Amber stopped, too. And when Lottie ran to greet Tom, Amber was right behind her.

Lottie barked and rolled over for Tom to tickle her tummy. Amber did the same.

"Hello, Lottie's little shadow!" Tom laughed and tickled Amber's tummy, too.

"I like that," purred Amber, rubbing the side of her cheek against Tom's hand.

Mrs. Bradman came into the kitchen. She opened some cans and put food into several bowls. Then she banged the fork on the side of a can, and Bracken arrived with some of Amber's brothers and sisters.

They went over to the bowls of cat food, but Amber followed Lottie to wait for the dog-food bowl.

"Mom," said Tom, putting the last dish of food down on the kitchen floor, "I think I've found someone else who'd like a kitten."

"Good," said Mrs. Bradman. "Who?"

Amber pricked up her ears and listened.

"The Green family down the street," said Tom. "It's Sam's ninth birthday next week and he's asked for a kitten. They've never had a cat before, only dogs, but they said they'd like to come over tomorrow and choose one. Is that all right?"

"Of course," said Mrs. Bradman.

"They'd better not choose me," meowed Amber, with her mouth full, as she moved closer to Lottie.

The next afternoon after school, Sam Green and his mother arrived at the Bradmans' house. Amber wasn't at all interested — until she noticed that they'd brought three dogs with them!

There was one that looked a little like Lottie, but with a shorter coat. And there was a white one, covered in black spots. And the third one was short — not much taller than Amber — but long and sausage-shaped.

"We thought the dogs should come," said Mrs. Green, as they came into the living room. "There's no point getting a cat that's terrified of dogs."

"And you'll have to make sure all the dogs are willing to live with a cat!" said Mrs. Bradman.

"Woof!" "Woof!" "Woof!" barked the three dogs as soon as they saw Bracken and her kittens. The cats bolted upstairs, hissing and spitting as they ran — except Amber.

She stayed beside Lottie who greeted the dogs with interest. They touched noses and walked around each other, sniffing and wagging their tails. Amber tried to do the same.

"That's amazing!" said Mrs. Green.

"Wow!" said Sam. "That kitten isn't afraid at all!"

Amber looked up, surprised. "Of course I'm not," she meowed.

"And she's so sweet!" said Mrs. Green, crouching down to get a closer look. "Have you given her a name?"

"We call her Amber," said Tom.

"Hmmm, it suits her. I think we'd call her that if we chose her," said Mrs. Green.

Sam nodded. "All the dogs seem to like her," he said. "And so do I!" He bent down to stroke the kitten. "Can we have her?"

"But I live here," meowed Amber, scampering away to hide behind Lottie.

A week later, Sam arrived with his father, carrying a large cardboard box with handles on the top. Amber had almost forgotten about his choosing her. She dashed into the kitchen. Lottie was lying across the mat in front of the stove.

"Don't tell them I'm here," Amber me-owed, and she burrowed under one of Lottie's front legs, hoping the golden retriever's coat would cover her.

She stayed as still as she could, but her heart was pounding so loudly she was sure everyone would notice her. She listened as Mrs. Brad-man brought Sam and Mr. Green into the kitchen.

Tom and Ellie ran in from the yard.

"Hello," said Tom. "Happy birthday! Have you come for Amber?"

"Yes," said Sam, fidgeting from one foot to the other. "I've been dying to come and get her all week."

"She was here a moment ago," said Mrs. Bradman. "I wonder where she went?"

"I went to the library," said Sam, as every-one searched for Amber. "And I borrowed loads of books on kittens. I know all about how to look after one now."

"That's good," said Mrs. Bradman, peering

under the kitchen table. "I'm glad you're going to look after her so well."

Not as well as Lottie does, thought Amber.

"And I have some birthday money," Sam went on. "I went to the pet store after school today and bought a special cat basket for her and a windup mouse and a little ball with a bell in it. Do you think she'll like them?"

"I'm sure she will," said Mrs. Bradman.

No I won't! thought Amber. *I've never played with cat toys. Only dog toys!*

"Now where is that kitten?" said Mrs. Bradman.

Mr. Green bent down to stroke Lottie. "Hello," he said. Then he began to smile. "What's this little thing, hidden in your fur?"

"You sneaky thing!" Tom laughed as he crouched down and lifted Amber very gently from her hiding place.

"She's very sweet!" said Mr. Green.

"I'm sure she'll be very happy with you," said Mrs. Bradman.

"But I want to stay with Lottie," meowed Amber.

At that moment, Bracken crept into the room and sat in a corner, far away from the dogs. Tom put Amber down next to her mom for a moment.

"Be good," said Bracken, licking Amber's nose. "You're going to be fine with three dogs to follow around!"

Before Amber could reply, Tom picked her up again for Ellie and Mrs. Bradman to say good-bye.

"Good-bye," she meowed sadly at each of them. Then she looked down at Lottie who was wagging her tail. "I'll really miss you," she meowed.

"And I'll miss you, too, my little friend," Lottie woofed, "but you've got some new doggy friends at Sam's house. You won't be lonely. Good luck!"

2

The first thing Amber saw when the box opened a few minutes later was a white face with black spots peering down at her. It was one of the Greens' dogs.

"Remember me?" she meowed.

"You're Lottie's little friend," woofed the dalmatian. "You've come to live with us, haven't you?"

"Out of the way, Jordan," Amber heard, as

Sam reached into the box and lifted her out. After giving her a quick cuddle, he put her down on the carpet.

Amber dashed up to Jordan. "So, are we going to be friends then?" she meowed nervously.

Mr. Green laughed. "This one certainly likes dogs!" he said.

Jordan bent down to give Amber a curious sniff. "Lottie told us you were unusual for a cat," he woofed.

Amber rubbed the side of her face against Jordan's long, bony legs. "I like you already," she purred.

"And you're a sweet little thing," Jordan woofed back.

Amber followed him into the kitchen. Everything looked very different at the Bradmans'. "Where are the other dogs?" she meowed.

"In the yard," woofed Jordan. "They'll be in soon."

If the other two are as friendly as Jordan, maybe

it won't be too bad here after all! Amber thought to herself.

Sam came into the kitchen, smiling and holding something in his hands. "Here you are, Amber," he said. "A windup mouse." He put the mouse on the floor in front of her.

Amber looked at it. It didn't smell like a mouse. She didn't trust it, so she began to back away.

Suddenly, the mouse made a strange whirring noise and started to skim across the kitchen floor. Amber arched her back as the mouse came toward her. "Get away from me!" she hissed and ran behind Jordan.

"Don't you like it?" asked Sam.

"Get away from me!" Amber hissed again as the mouse came nearer, but at last it slowed down and stopped.

Sam picked it up. "Oh, no," he said. "I bought it just for you. I thought all cats liked toys like this."

"Well, I don't," meowed Amber. "I'd rather play with Jordan."

But Sam didn't seem to understand. "I've got some more toys," he said. "And a basket for you. Let's try that." He picked Amber up and placed her in the new basket.

Amber didn't feel as comfortable in there as she had in Lottie's basket. It didn't smell right and she didn't want to stay in it.

Just then she heard a scratching sound on the back door. Sam went to open it and, while he wasn't looking, Amber jumped out of the uncomfortable basket.

A Labrador ran in. "Hey, Buster!" said Sam.

Buster skidded to a stop and sniffed Amber. "Remember me?" she meowed.

"Of course," barked Buster, and he licked her nose. It reminded Amber of Lottie and made her feel much more at home.

And then the third dog galloped into the kitchen, yapping loudly. "Hi, Laddie," said Sam. "Come and say hello to the new kitten."

"Oh, you're here at last!" yapped Laddie, giving her a friendly sniff. Laddie, a small, red dachshund, was low enough for Amber to sniff back. That made her very happy!

For the rest of the evening, Amber followed the three dogs around. She played with them, ate with them, and that night, she went to sleep curled up with Buster, the golden Labrador. As she fell asleep under one of Buster's gentle paws, Amber realized she was having too much fun to miss Lottie.

The next morning, Amber woke when Tom pushed the Greens' newspaper through the mailbox. She heard Sam running downstairs to open the front door and scampered into the hall to see her old friend.

"Hello, Amber!" Tom said. "Have you settled in okay?"

"Yes, thanks," meowed Amber.

"She's fine," said Sam, "thanks to the dogs! But she isn't interested in the cat toys or the new basket I bought her."

Tom laughed. "We always said that Amber thinks she's a dog!" he said.

Just then Buster ran into the hall, took the newspaper in his mouth, and ran back into the kitchen to give it to Mr. Green. Amber ran after him and returned a few moments later, dragging part of the paper behind her.

"Hey, look at that!" laughed Sam. "She even wants to carry the paper!"

Tom laughed, too.

Amber dropped the pages of the newspaper she was carrying. Why were they laughing at her? "I'll practice," she meowed. "Then you'll see — I can be just like a dog."

When Tom arrived to deliver the newspaper the next day, Amber was waiting on the mat. She had a piece of paper in her mouth.

Tom peeped through the mailbox and saw her. "You're a smart kitten!" he laughed. Amber purred. She liked being praised.

Soon after breakfast, Mrs. Green opened the back door and let all three dogs into the yard.

Amber was just about to sneak out with them when Mr. Green stopped her. "No, Amber," he said. "You can't go out there yet." He closed the door firmly.

Amber sat on the mat and looked up at him. "Why not?" she meowed.

But Mr. Green hurried off. He was late for work.

Amber jumped up onto the windowsill to watch Jordan, Buster, and Laddie running around the yard. "Are you having a good time?" she meowed, but they didn't seem to hear her.

When Sam came downstairs for breakfast, he ran over to Amber and picked her up. He held her gently against his chest. "You can go out in the yard when you're older," he said, stroking the back of Amber's head. "After you've had your shots."

"Shots?" Amber meowed.

"All cats have them when they're nine weeks old and twelve weeks old," Sam said. "It's to stop you from getting sick. Your first one's today, at the vet's."

When Sam lifted Amber into the cardboard cat carrier that afternoon, Amber felt frightened. She didn't know what to expect when she got to the vet's.

But the vet had a kind face and a soft voice. Amber soon forgot her fear. She was so busy looking around the strange new place that she hardly noticed the tiny prick on her neck.

"That wasn't so bad, was it?" the vet said, smiling.

"Oh! Was that it?" meowed Amber, as Sam placed her back in the cat carrier.

*　　*　　*

Over the next few weeks, Amber learned to roll over and play dead, chase balls, and carry bigger and bigger pieces of paper in her mouth. But she was dying to play out in the yard.

It seemed such a long time, waiting to be twelve weeks old!

At last, Amber had her second shot. And the next day, when the dogs were let out into the yard, Amber was allowed out, too. "Wait for me!" she meowed as they all tumbled out and raced on the grass. But the dogs weren't used to having Amber outside with them, and they soon forgot about her.

Amber stood by the step and looked around. Now that she was in it, the yard seemed enormous! She stepped onto the grass. It was soft and wet.

She walked through it, slowly at first. Then she grew braver. She began to run. There was so much to explore!

Soon she was following Buster, Laddie, and Jordan as they raced around.

It was the most fun she had ever had!

Later on when Sam came home from school, he ran into the yard to play with them. He threw sticks for them to chase. Amber did her best to reach the sticks first, but her tiny legs didn't carry her fast enough.

Sam saw what was happening. He called the

dogs to heel, then threw a tiny stick, just for Amber.

Amber ran after it, picked it up, brought it back, and dropped it at Sam's feet.

"Good job!" he laughed.

"I'm getting more like a dog every day!" Amber meowed proudly.

She raced off after the dogs, who had gone to see what Mr. Green was doing. He had cut a hole in the back door and was fixing a flap over it.

"That's for you, Amber," he said, showing her how to use it with his hand.

"Try it."

Cautiously, Amber pushed her nose against the flap. It moved, so that she could walk through the hole into the kitchen. She turned around and came back out into the yard. "That's great!" she meowed. "Now I can go in and out whenever I want!"

* * *

The following morning, Amber saw the dogs sitting by the front door. It was time for Sam to walk to school and, usually, Mrs. Green and the dogs kept him company.

Amber got excited. Now that she'd been outside, perhaps she'd be allowed to go, too. She went and sat beside him.

"Not you, Amber," Sam said. "Cats don't go for walks. Besides," he smiled, "we only have three leashes!" He clipped them onto the dogs' collars.

After they had left, Amber walked sadly into the living room and leaped onto an armchair. She'd have a snooze while they were out, she decided. The only good thing about being a cat was being allowed to sleep on the furniture! That was something the dogs weren't allowed to do!

But then Amber remembered her new cat flap. *I could sneak out and follow them!* she thought excitedly.

Amber leaped out of the chair and ran into

the kitchen. She pushed her way through the cat flap and sped through the backyard. She could hear Laddie yapping to the other two as usual, and followed the noise.

Climbing over the fence, Amber raced through an alley that led to Liberty Street. She was just in time to see Mrs. Green, Sam, and the dogs turning the corner.

Amber raced after them. What an adventure! She had never gone farther than the yard before. Her heart was racing with excitement, but she felt nervous, too. There were so many different sounds and smells.

Keeping close to the bushes and walls, Amber followed the dogs along Liberty Street and around the corner onto a busier street. The noise of the traffic and the bustle of so many people almost made her turn back. *But if I want to be a dog, I'll have to act like one,* she thought. *Buster, Jordan, and Laddie are brave and so am I!*

Mrs. Green and Sam came to a part of the

street that was striped. Amber watched them stop, then walk across the stripes to get to the other side. She was just about to follow when she heard her name.

"Amber? It is Amber, isn't it?"

Amber looked up at the lady who had spoken to her. It was Tom Bradman's grandma, Mrs. Jennings, wearing her big, white coat. Mrs. Jennings was a crossing guard. She stopped the traffic with a big sign, so children on their way to school could cross the street.

"Yes," meowed Amber. "Only I'm trying to be a dog."

"You shouldn't be out on your own," said Mrs. Jennings. She looked across the street at Sam and Mrs. Green.

"I'm trying to catch up to them," meowed Amber, "so I can go for a walk with them."

"Mrs. Green!" called Mrs. Jennings. "Sam!"

Mrs. Green and Sam turned around and saw Amber. "Oh, no!" Amber heard Sam shout worriedly. "Amber shouldn't be here by the main road — it's dangerous!"

"I'll take her home if you like," called Mrs. Jennings. "I finish here in a couple of minutes."

"Thanks," called Mrs. Green. "I'd be very grateful. My husband's home to answer the door."

But Amber wanted to do things by herself. So before Mrs. Jennings could pick her up, she darted away, back along the busy street to Liberty Street.

A black kitten appeared from inside the store on the corner. It was Jet, Amber's brother.

"Hello, Jet," Amber meowed. "Do you live here?"

"Yes," meowed Jet. "What have you been doing?"

"I was trying to be a dog and go for a walk," meowed Amber. "But I didn't get very far. I'm on my way home."

A dark gray kitten walked down from some steps nearby and came to join in the conversation. It was their sister, Emerald, who also lived on Liberty Street.

"Hello, Emerald," meowed Amber. She was really pleased to see her brother and sister. But before they could talk anymore, Amber saw Mrs. Jennings coming to look for her. Not wanting to get into more trouble, she ran home.

3

A few minutes later, Amber sat in Laddie's box feeling very sorry for herself. After speaking with Mrs. Jennings, Mr. Green had firmly locked the cat flap.

"I hate being a cat!" Amber meowed. "Why can't I be a dog?" She thought about Jet and Emerald. They seemed to like being cats. Amber couldn't imagine why.

The cat flap stayed locked the next time her

friends went out for a walk. And the next time. In fact, the Greens seemed determined to stop her from going with them. Amber was really upset. *Will I ever be able to go for a walk, like a dog?* she wondered.

Her chance came sooner than she expected. One Saturday afternoon, the Greens forgot to lock the cat flap. Amber waited for them to leave, then she ran straight through the cat flap, over the backyard fence, and down the alley onto Liberty Street.

The Greens weren't walking toward Sam's school this time — they were going the other way. Amber followed them, staying hidden by jumping from yard to yard down the street.

Soon they came to the edge of town. All Amber could see ahead was open green space. *Wow!* she thought.

Sam let the dogs off their leashes and they ran off. This open countryside was a new experience for Amber and her heart beat fast. She wanted to stop and sniff everything and explore this new place. But more than that, she wanted to play in all this space with Buster, Jordan, and Laddie.

Suddenly, she heard Laddie bark and he came running toward her, followed by Buster and Jordan. The three dogs ran rings around Amber, barking loudly.

"Shh!" meowed Amber. "Don't let them know I'm here."

But it was too late. Sam came running over. "What have you found?" he called to the dogs. "A rabbit?"

He stopped and stared. "Oh, no!" he cried. "Mom, Dad! Who forgot to lock the cat flap?"

"We'll have to go back," said Mrs. Green when she saw the naughty kitten.

Mr. Green nodded. "We can't have her following us any farther."

"Why not?" meowed Amber. "I'm not any trouble."

"Why not?" asked Sam. "She does everything else that dogs do, so why can't she come for a walk?"

"Thanks, Sam!" meowed Amber. "That's what I've been waiting to hear!"

Mrs. Green laughed. "Oh, all right," she said. "That cat's so determined to be a dog!"

Amber was glad she didn't have to stay hidden anymore. It was wonderful to race through the fields with her three friends. But when they came to a farm, Sam picked her up. "We have to walk more slowly through here," he said. "So we don't frighten the animals."

Mr. and Mrs. Green kept Buster, Jordan, and Laddie on their leashes until they came to open fields again. Then Sam put Amber down to run with the dogs.

All of a sudden, Amber heard a snort. What's that? She turned to look and froze with surprise. An enormous brown animal was staring fiercely at them. It had wild brown eyes, a big ring through its nose, and two very sharp-looking horns!

Mrs. Green screamed.

"A bull!" shouted Mr. Green. "Run!"

"What's a bull?" Amber meowed. But everyone had started running. Mr. Green led the way across the field, pulling Mrs. Green by the hand. Mrs. Green had grabbed Sam and was dragging him along behind her. The dogs ran speedily ahead of them toward the gate at the side of the field.

"Come on, Amber," Sam shouted over his shoulder.

But the bull had caught up to Amber and stood in her way. "You don't seem very friendly," she meowed nervously.

"I'm not!" roared the bull.

Amber began to tremble. "Help!" she meowed. Then, out of the corner of her eye, she noticed a tree nearby. *I can climb that!* she thought. The bull took its eyes off her to watch the others as they climbed the fence to safety. Amber took her chance. She ran away from it and began to haul herself up the tree,

faster than she'd ever climbed before. *Quick,*
quick, she said to herself, as she dug her claws
into the bark.

Amber was halfway up the trunk when the
bull turned back and saw she was gone. With
a roar that echoed through the branches, it
lost interest and walked off to the other end of
the field.

Thank goodness I'm a cat! Amber thought for
the first time ever. *Dogs can't climb trees!*

Checking that the bull wasn't looking, Amber jumped down from the tree. Then making
herself as low as possible to the ground, she
scuttled across the field to the fence to join
the others. "Hello!" she meowed.

"Amber!" Sam cried. "You're safe!"

"I thought the bull must have gotten you!"
barked Jordan.

"It's a good thing cats can climb trees!" said
Mrs. Green. "That must have saved your life,
Amber!"

"I know!" meowed Amber.

"Come on," said Mr. Green. "Let's go home."

They had almost reached their house on Liberty Street when a black kitten jumped down from a wall in front of them. Amber heard Mrs. Green gasp.

"Oh! It made me jump!" she said. "My nerves are shattered from that bull!"

But Amber knew who it was. "Hello, Jet," she meowed. "We've just had a great adventure."

"So you managed to go on your walk!" meowed Jet.

The kittens touched noses, and Amber told Jet about the bull and how she had climbed the tree to escape from it.

"Good job," purred Jet. "Now, perhaps you'll agree that being a cat is best!"

"Hmmm," Amber meowed. "Maybe you're right!"

Jet

1

Jet sat in the doorway of the corner grocery store in the warm sunshine. It was the best place to be if you wanted to see everything that was going on. And Jet did!

Mrs. Jennings was walking toward him along the sidewalk. Jet was used to watching Mrs. Jennings out on the busy street, helping children to cross on their way to school. She would walk onto the striped part of the street, hold her sign up, and stop the cars.

Mrs. Jennings always walked past the corner grocery store at the same time on her way home. "Hello, Jet!" she said when she reached him. "Are you looking after the store?"

Jet stood up and rubbed the side of his face against Mrs. Jennings's legs. "Of course I am," he meowed. "They always need my help."

"You're such a handsome boy," said Mrs. Jennings as she bent to stroke his gleaming black coat. Then she chuckled. "Black cats are very common," she said, "but you're the only one I've ever met with a pure white tip on your tail!"

"Thank you," purred Jet. He was proud of that white tip. Lots of people admired it.

"I've just got to run into the store for a loaf of bread," said Mrs. Jennings. "Are you coming?"

Jet followed Mrs. Jennings through the open door and into the store. He jumped up onto the counter by a pile of fresh bread. But immediately, two strong hands lifted him down again.

Jet looked up to see who had put him back on the floor. It was Steve. He and Angie, his wife, ran the corner grocery store. Jet had come to live with them when he'd left the Bradmans' house as a tiny kitten.

"I don't mind you being up with the cans and boxes, Jet," Steve said firmly, "but you know you shouldn't be near the fresh food."

"Sorry!" Jet meowed. Steve had told him several times, but he kept forgetting. "I was only trying to help." He rubbed against Steve's ankles. "Are we still friends?"

Steve smiled down at Jet, then grinned at Mrs. Jennings. He was always smiling and friendly. Jet loved him.

Mrs. Jennings smiled back. "It seems like only yesterday that Jet was one of Bracken's newborn kittens," she said. Jet's mom, Bracken, lived nearby on Liberty Street with Mrs. Jennings's daughter and her family.

Just then Angie came into the store from the room at the back. "I know," she said, "but Jet's almost a year old now! I remember Tom was so excited when he came into the store to get the newspapers on the morning Bracken's kittens were born. It made us want to have one." Tom was Mrs. Jennings's grandson, and he delivered newspapers for Angie and Steve.

Jet listened to Angie talking. He loved her high, singsong voice.

When Angie and Steve had brought Jet to his new home many months ago, he'd had a wonderful surprise. He remembered the first time he had explored the shelves and closets, with their exciting smells. And he still found new corners to explore and boxes to sniff.

Then when Jet was twelve weeks old, Steve had put a cat flap in the side entrance to the store, where the deliveries were made. It meant that Jet could come and go as he pleased. It was a great place to live!

Mrs. Jennings paid for her loaf of bread.

"Oh, I forgot to ask," she said to Angie as she headed for the door. "How are you?"

"Very well, thanks," said Angie. "But I seem to be getting bigger every day!" she laughed.

She has become rather plump lately! Jet thought to himself.

The next morning, when Tom Bradman collected his newspapers to deliver, Jet helped him load his bag.

"Get out of the bag, Jet!" Tom laughed.

"But you like me helping you," Jet meowed.

Tom picked him up for a moment and gave him a cuddle.

"I remember you coming to get the papers on the first morning I was here," Jet purred. "I was afraid you'd come to take me away from Angie and Steve. But once I knew I could stay in my nice new home, I was really happy to see you."

Tom put Jet down and picked up his heavy

bag. "See you tomorrow," he said as he left the shop.

"I look forward to it!" Jet meowed. But before he saw Tom again, he had the rest of the day to enjoy. He couldn't wait to meet today's customers. They would pet him and admire his silky black coat and comment on his unusual white-tipped tail. It was great being the star attraction!

"Oh, no!"

Just then Jet heard Angie's voice, much higher and louder than usual, coming from the storeroom behind the store. He walked over to see what was the matter.

"What's up?" asked Steve, who had hurried downstairs from their apartment above the shop.

"Look!" cried Angie, pointing at a corner behind some boxes. "Mouse droppings!"

Steve and Jet went to investigate. Jet sniffed around the corner and his whiskers twitched with excitement. *Ooh, where's that mouse? I'd love it for my dinner!* he thought.

"It's even nibbled the cheese without getting caught!" said Angie. Steve had put down a trap to try and catch the mouse.

Steve sighed. "I'd better try again," he said as Angie sat down on the steps. "We'll be in trouble from the health inspector if we have mice in the store."

Angie looked upset and Jet hated to see her worried.

"Sorry!" said Steve, bending to kiss her. "I'll set the trap again tonight."

"And I'll see what I can do," meowed Jet.

"You go and take a nap, Angie," said Steve gently. "I'll manage the store this morning."

"Thanks, I get so tired right now," she said with a smile. "Call me if you need me."

Jet watched Angie heave herself up from the steps and waddle to the stairs. She really had gotten bigger lately!

After she had gone upstairs, Steve went into the store. Jet stayed behind to prowl, looking for the mouse. The scent of the mouse was very strong. But there was no sign of it.

Just then Jet heard Mrs. Jennings's voice in the store. She must be on her way to work at the school crossing. "I'll catch you later, mouse," Jet hissed, then he ran into the store to greet his friend.

Very early the next morning, Jet trotted upstairs before Angie and Steve were awake. Their bedroom door was shut, so he sat outside and called. "Wake up," he yowled. "Open the door. I've got a surprise for you."

"Whatever's wrong with Jet?" he heard Angie say.

"I've got something to show you!" meowed Jet, lifting his paw to scratch at the door.

The door opened. Steve stood there, half-dressed, blinking in the darkness of the landing. "What is it, Jet?" he asked.

"You wanted that mouse caught," said Jet. "So here it is!"

"Hey, Angie!" Steve called. "He's caught the mouse. Good job, you smart cat!"

He lifted Jet with the mouse still in his mouth for Angie to see. "Great!" said Angie, who was sitting up in bed. "You're better than any mousetrap, Jet. I'll call you 'Chief Mouser'!"

"Thanks!" meowed Jet proudly. "I like that!"

Grinning, Steve took the mouse from Jet and carried it downstairs. "I'll put it outside the side door for you," he said.

Half an hour later, when Tom came to collect the newspapers for his round, Jet was walking around the store with his head and tail held high.

"You look pleased with yourself," said Tom. "What have you been up to?"

"I'm Chief Mouser!" meowed Jet.

"He caught a mouse during the night," said Steve. "He's Chief Mouser from now on."

Jet couldn't wait for it to get dark so that he

could try to catch another mouse. He had smelled mice before, behind the store and under the steps that led up to the apartments next door. His sister Emerald lived in one of the apartments with George. *Perhaps she can be my Assistant Mouser!* Jet thought.

Emerald came by the corner grocery later that day to say hello to Jet.

"What do you think?" meowed Jet after he had told his sister his plan.

"I'd love to be Assistant Mouser," Emerald replied. "I could do it with some practice."

So that night, Jet and Emerald prowled the area. When Jet brought home his share of the catch, Angie and Steve were delighted.

"Good job!" Angie said when Jet presented them with the mice.

Later that afternoon, Mrs. Bradman, Tom's mom, came into the store on her way home from work. "It's wonderful to see all our kittens growing up into such handsome cats," she said, picking Jet up and stroking him.

"Not just handsome . . ." said Angie.

". . . like his owner . . ." added Steve.

". . . but clever, too . . . !" said Angie, grinning at her husband.

". . . unlike his owner!" finished Steve roaring with laughter.

Laughing, too, Angie explained. "What Steve means," she said, "is that Jet is better at catching mice than he is!"

"Great work, Jet!" said Mrs. Bradman, tickling the sides of Jet's face. "Our Bracken will be so proud when I tell her."

2

The next day, a boy and his mom came into the store. His mom also had a baby in a stroller. Jet decided to hide behind a box. The boy looked all right, but Jet wasn't sure if he liked babies. This one was making lots of strange gurgling noises!

"Hello, Sue. How are you?" said Angie, leaning over the counter to look at the baby. "And how's little Hannah?"

"We're really good, thanks," said Sue. "And how about you?"

"Fine," smiled Angie. "Aside from looking like a balloon!"

"How much longer now?" asked Sue.

"Just a couple of weeks," said Angie.

While his mom and Angie were talking, the boy explored the store and noticed Jet behind his box. "Hello, kitty!" he said, bending to stroke the kitten. "Are you hiding?"

Jet began to purr, enjoying the attention. "Not from you," he meowed. "I like you! But I'm not quite sure about your baby sister yet. She seems a bit scary!"

"Da da da da da," Hannah said loudly. Jet crouched lower behind the box.

"Colin!" the boy's mom called. "Come and help choose a birthday card for Dad."

Colin hurried over to the counter where the greeting cards were displayed.

Jet followed, creeping nearer to Hannah,

who was banging a toy against the stroller with a big smile on her face.

"Where's Steve this morning?" Sue asked Angie.

"In the back, sorting out a delivery that's just come in," said Angie.

Sue nodded. "Now, what do I want?" she said. "Let me see. A loaf of bread, a can of baked beans, and some eggs."

"Ga ga ga, ga ga GAAA!" said Hannah even louder.

Jet dashed back behind his box, deciding babies were very scary. He watched in surprise as Angie smiled and wiggled her finger at Hannah while Sue got the groceries she needed. Angie seemed to like babies.

Then Hannah began to make soft gurgling sounds instead. Jet didn't mind those so much, so he decided to take another look. He poked his head out from behind the box, watching Hannah carefully, in case she started to make frightening noises again.

Hannah noticed him and pointed her finger. "Goo goo, gurgle gurgle," she said softly.

Jet began to feel less afraid. He crawled forward a little. *Perhaps she wants to be friends,* he thought.

"I think Hannah likes you, Jet," said Angie from behind the counter.

Sue came back with a basketful of food, and Angie began ringing it up on the cash register.

"Da da da da da da da," said Hannah, waving her arms above her head.

The baby's noise was getting loud again, so Jet stepped back a little, still watching. Then he crept forward, curious to see more. "You're a strange creature," he meowed.

"Ga ga ga ga ga ga," Hannah burbled. Then she put her fingers in her mouth and began to chew them.

Angie and Sue were busy chatting and laughing. And Colin was still looking at the birthday cards for dads.

Jet walked around Hannah's stroller, looking at her. She chuckled, kicking her legs and clapping her hands. He sniffed the air. She had a different kind of scent, a sweet smell that reminded Jet of when Angie had a bath.

"Da da da da da da," said Hannah again, pointing her chubby finger and waving her arms.

Slowly Jet grew used to the baby's movements and noises. She didn't seem to want to hurt him. Perhaps he could get near enough for her to stroke him. Then they could be friends.

He pushed his nose against the stroller, then rubbed the side of his face along it, letting Hannah touch him.

Hannah squealed loudly with delight. Frightened, Jet backed away. But then she became quiet again, so he couldn't resist creeping closer.

The baby reached out her arms and ruffled Jet's fur with her tiny hands. It felt nice!

"You're not as scary as I thought," Jet meowed.

"Goo goo goo goo," Hannah cooed as she poked Jet's ears, then touched his long white whiskers.

He began to walk around and around the stroller. Hannah swiveled around as Jet went by and she stretched out to touch him, giggling. *I'm beginning to like this strange little person!* Jet thought.

Then, suddenly, Hannah lunged toward him.

Her tiny hand grasped the white tip of his tail. Jet felt the grip tighten. "Da da da da da da!" she shouted and she pulled Jet's tail as hard as she could!

"Owww!" yowled Jet as a sharp pain shot up his back. "Let go!" he hissed. "Let go! Yowww!"

As suddenly as she had grabbed the tail, Hannah let go. She threw herself against the back of her stroller, opened her mouth very wide, and screamed. "Wa wa wa wa wa wa!"

Frightened out of his wits, Jet leaped up onto the counter, his back arched and his fur standing on end. "How dare you pull my tail!" he hissed at the baby. "It really hurt!"

Sue and Angie stopped talking, and Colin dropped the pile of cards he was holding.

"Jet!" Angie cried, shocked.

Sue lifted Hannah out of the stroller and began rocking her. "Your cat attacked Hannah!" she shouted at Angie. Hannah's screaming grew louder.

Angie looked at Jet as if she couldn't believe it. "But Jet's such a good-natured cat," she said.

"Yes, Mom," Colin agreed. "I was stroking that kitten earlier — he's really gentle."

"Well, he'd better not have scratched her!" shouted Sue. "There, there," she said in a high voice as she inspected Hannah. "Did that nasty cat go after you?"

"Wa wa wa wa wa wa," went the baby.

She turned on Angie. "You need to control that cat!" she said.

"I've never seen Jet hiss like that before," Angie argued back. "Hannah must have frightened him!"

Jet looked down at the angry women. *They're both very annoyed and it's all my fault. Maybe I shouldn't have hissed like that.* He turned his head to inspect the tip of his tail. *But she really hurt me!*

Just then the door opened at the back of the shop and Steve rushed in.

"What's going on?" he asked.

"Your cat attacked Hannah," Sue said.

"He didn't!" shouted Angie, whose face had become red. "Hannah frightened him!"

"Calm down, honey," Steve said, putting his arm around Angie. "It's not good for you to get so worked up."

"Hannah was only playing!" shouted Sue.

"But, Mom!" Colin said, bending down to pick up the cards he'd dropped. "You know how hard Hannah sometimes pulls our hair when she's playing. Perhaps she did the same thing to the kitten."

"Yes, yes!" meowed Jet from his hiding place on the counter. "You're right!"

"That's different!" shouted Colin's mom. Then Hannah started crying so loudly that no one could hear themselves think.

"Now, now," said Steve hurriedly. "Let's drop it, then Sue can pay for her groceries and go home."

"Pay for my groceries?" Sue said angrily.

"I'm not buying anything from here, thank you!"

She put the still-screaming Hannah back in the stroller and stormed out of the store, calling, "Come on, Colin — we're late!"

As soon as the baby had gone, Jet jumped down from the counter. Colin gave a sheepish smile to Angie and Steve, then petted Jet and followed his mom.

"Thanks for sticking up for me!" Jet purred after him. Then he ran around the counter to Angie and Steve. "I didn't mean to upset that baby," he meowed, "but she hurt me."

Angie and Steve didn't seem to hear him, so he rubbed the side of his face against Angie's legs, but instead of stroking him as usual, she began to cry. "Sue didn't have to be so nasty," she said.

"It's okay. She was just worried about Hannah," Steve said, hugging her. "Now you must calm down."

Jet wrapped himself around Angie's legs, but

she was too busy wiping her eyes to notice him. "Come on, let's put these groceries back where they belong," she said, taking a deep breath.

Normally, Angie and Steve would have let Jet help them, but their usual cheery faces looked sad and they were only interested in putting everything away. They seemed to have forgotten all about him. He watched them return the unwanted food to the shelves, then crept silently out the door and onto the street.

They've lost a customer because of me. No wonder they were upset! Jet thought.

Emerald was sitting in a corner at the bottom of the steps that led up to the apartments. Jet didn't see her at first because she was hidden in the shadows. But when she turned to talk to him he saw her emerald eyes glinting. "Hello," she meowed. "You look miserable."

"I am," meowed Jet sadly. "Angie and Steve are angry with me. They don't want to talk to me anymore."

"Why? What have you done?" meowed Emerald.

When Jet had told her about Hannah, Emerald stood up and walked over to him. She rubbed her nose against his. "I'm sure they're not really upset with you," she meowed. "It's not like them to be angry with anyone!"

"I know," meowed Jet. "That's why I'm so unhappy. They've always been so kind to me. The last thing I want to do is upset them."

Just then the front door at the top of the steps opened. The two kittens looked up. "Emerald, dinnertime!" It was George, Emerald's owner.

"I've got to go," said Emerald, scampering up the steps. "Don't worry!"

"I'll try not to," meowed Jet after his sister had gone indoors. "But what if Angie and Steve never forgive me?"

He curled up sadly and put his head on his paws. He just couldn't bear the thought of it.

3

Jet didn't go home until evening. He thought it was best to stay out of Angie's and Steve's way. But when the sun started to go down, he felt hungry.

He went to the side entrance and pushed the cat flap with his nose. There was no sign of Angie or Steve, but a dish of cat food had been left there for him. He jumped inside and began to eat hungrily. *Perhaps they're not too upset with me,* he thought to himself.

When he had finished the food, Jet crept over to the stairs that led up to the apartment. The living room door was open a crack and he could see the light was on. *Angie and Steve must be in there,* he thought.

"I'm so uncomfortable." Angie's voice floated down the stairs. She didn't sound angry anymore! But she didn't sound her usual happy self, either. Jet thought he would leave them alone for a while longer. The mice would be coming out now that it was getting dark. He would go and see if he could catch any.

Jet spent a long time sniffing around the front of the store. There didn't seem to be any mice around. He began to feel sleepy, and so he went inside to look for somewhere to curl up. He found an empty cardboard box and jumped in. Usually, he curled up in his basket in the kitchen, but he decided to leave it until the morning and go upstairs. Surely, Angie and Steve would forgive him by the morning.

He didn't feel like he'd been asleep for long when he heard Tom arriving to get his newspapers. Jet peeked into the store. Steve was rushing around, sorting the papers, and filling the delivery bags. Usually, Jet would have jumped up to help Steve, but he thought he would let him do it on his own today.

"Hello, Jet," said Tom, noticing him. "You're quiet this morning."

"Steve's not very pleased with me," meowed Jet.

Just then, Angie called from upstairs. "Steve! Come quickly!" Her voice was shrill.

What's the matter with Angie? Jet thought. *What could be so urgent?*

"I'm coming," Steve shouted. He hurriedly handed Tom his full bag, and then ran up the stairs two at a time without stopping to talk to Jet.

"Good luck," shouted Tom as he left the store.

Everything's different this morning! Jet couldn't believe everyone had left him in the store on his own. Then he had another surprise. Steve came running back down the stairs, carrying a suitcase.

Jet couldn't understand it. The last time Jet had seen Steve carrying a bag like that he and Angie had gone away for a week. *But they told me about it first,* Jet thought. *And they left someone to look after the store and feed me!*

"I'll get the car out," Steve called up the stairs and then he dashed out of the store.

"All right," Angie called back. Her voice sounded very strange! She was coming down the stairs very slowly. She had a deep frown on her face and she kept stopping to hold on to the banisters.

"What's wrong?" meowed Jet.

"Not now, Jet," Angie said, not even looking at him. She held her hand under her big tummy as she walked past him and out the door. Then she switched off the lights and turned the key in the lock!

Jet heard the *vroom vroom* of the car engine starting, then doors slamming, and the car driving away. He just couldn't understand it. He sat still for a while and then washed himself while he thought. He would go outside and see if there were any clues.

He jumped out through the cat flap and went around to the front of the store on Liberty Street. But nothing looked any different. Jet just couldn't understand it.

He watched people come up to the grocery store then walk away shaking their heads when they found it closed. "I don't know what's going on, either!" Jet meowed after them.

While Jet was stretched out in a front yard halfway down the street, a golden tabby came up to him. It was his sister Amber.

"Emerald tells me you're in trouble with your owners," she meowed.

"Yes, and now they've gone away," meowed Jet.

"Gone away?" meowed Amber, sitting down beside him. "Where to?"

When Jet had told Amber the whole story, she nuzzled gently against his face. "Emerald also told me Angie named you her Chief Mouser," she meowed. "Why don't you see if you can catch some mice to show them when they come home? They'd like that, wouldn't they?"

"Good idea. Will you help me?" Jet meowed, feeling a bit more cheerful. But secretly he was worried that Angie and Steve weren't coming home. What if they hadn't forgiven him for upsetting the baby?

It was dark when Jet heard the familiar sound of Steve's car coming down the street. He sat waiting inside the store with several mice that he and Amber had caught together. A key turned in the lock, Steve pushed open the door, and switched on the light. But where was Angie?

"I've brought you some presents," Jet me-owed.

Steve bent and stroked his head. "Good boy," he said with a smile. Jet was so glad to see that smile! Steve didn't seem upset anymore, but he didn't pick him up or pay him any more attention. He just put the dead mice outside the side door, then ran upstairs. Jet could hear him singing. *But why does Steve sound so happy if Angie isn't here?* Jet wondered.

The door opened and two men came in. "Steve!" they called. Jet heard Steve's feet thundering down the stairs.

"Hello!" Steve said as he ran into the shop.

"We just heard the news," said one of the men. "All the best!"

What news?

"Congratulations!" said the other man. He patted Steve on the back and Steve laughed.

Jet looked from one to the other. *What's going on? Why are they congratulating Steve?* He felt very confused.

All through the next day, lots more people came into the store, laughing and joking and thumping Steve on the back. But no one seemed to notice Jet. *It's almost as if I've become invisible!* he thought sadly. *I wish Angie would come back.*

The only person to pay him any attention all day was Colin. He walked past the store with his dad when Jet was sitting on the sidewalk washing his paws.

"I know you didn't hurt my baby sister," he said, bending down to stroke Jet.

"Thanks," Jet purred loudly, and Colin ran off to catch up with his dad.

That evening, after Steve closed the store, he drove away in the car again. But this time Jet didn't have to wait so long for him to return. He was sitting on the sidewalk outside the store doorway when the car stopped next to the curb. And there, sitting in the back of the car, was Angie!

Steve opened the car door and Angie climbed out. Her fat tummy had gone away and she was carrying a white bundle in her arms. *What's in there?* Jet wondered.

Steve opened the store door, and they went inside and up the stairs to their apartment. Jet followed. He wanted to know what they had brought home.

When they reached the living room, Angie sat down on the sofa and unwrapped the white bundle. Jet stood staring in amazement. It was pink and small with a wrinkled face . . . it was a baby! He couldn't believe that Angie and Steve had brought a baby home.

Jet flattened his ears and scuttled to the safety of the sideboard. There was just enough room for him to squeeze underneath it. He pressed his nose against the wall at the back of the sideboard, hoping that Angie and Steve wouldn't notice him.

But he'd forgotten to tuck in his tail!

"Come out of there, Jet, you silly thing!"

117

said Steve. "I can see the white tip of your tail." He spoke in such a friendly voice that Jet backed out from his hiding place.

Steve picked Jet up and held him against his chest. Jet nuzzled against him and smelled his familiar scent. He was beginning to feel better now that Steve was behaving more like his old self.

"Jet, this is the new member of our family," Steve said. "She's a little girl."

"I hope Jet gets along with her," said Angie anxiously.

Jet looked over at the tiny baby in her arms, his whiskers twitching. "I'll like anything if it means you won't disappear again," he meowed. "But I'd prefer it if she doesn't pull my tail!"

As Steve carried him closer to the sofa, Jet dug his claws into his sweater. He still wasn't sure if he wanted to go near the baby. Steve sat down next to Angie and gently unhooked Jet's claws. "Calm down, boy," he said with a big smile. "Don't worry. This baby's not going to hurt you."

Jet began to feel happy again. Angie and Steve still wanted him after all.

Angie reached over to stroke him. "Poor old Jet," she said. "First you have the fright of your life when your tail is pulled. Then we're too busy getting me off to the hospital to notice you. No wonder you're not sure what to make of it all."

"I have been a bit worried. But everything's okay now that you're home again," Jet purred. He looked at the baby lying asleep in Angie's arms. Then he gingerly stepped off Steve's lap onto the sofa. Slowly, he crept toward the baby. She certainly looked harmless.

Suddenly, the baby stirred, opened her eyes, and let out a cry. In a split second, Jet had shot off the sofa and was sliding under the sideboard. But Angie's soft voice stopped him in his tracks.

"Jet," she called. "Come back. Don't be

frightened. Just because the baby cries doesn't mean she's going to hurt you."

Jet turned around and looked at Angie. The baby was still crying. Jet wasn't sure. But then Angie lifted the baby up to her shoulder. And as if by magic the crying stopped.

"Come on, Jet — you're not scared, are you? You're the brave Chief Mouser of the house," said Steve, patting his lap for the kitten to climb up.

He's right, thought Jet. *I'm not scared of mice,*

so why should I be afraid of a baby? He jumped onto Steve's lap, then stepped next to Angie and peered at the baby. She had her eyes closed and was breathing noisily. Jet noticed that she smelled just like Angie. That was nice! Nice and comforting.

Jet nuzzled into Angie's arm, purring. "I think I'll like your baby," he meowed to Angie and Steve, flicking his white-tipped tail. "And perhaps I can teach her to leave my tail alone!"